Twinkle, Twinkle, Little Star

Twinkle, Twinkle Little Star

As told and illustrated by
Iza Trapani

WHISPERING COYOTE PRESS, INC.
Dallas

A special thanks to Anne Marie for opening the door,
and to Lou for letting me in.

Published by Whispering Coyote Press
300 Crescent Court, Suite 860 Dallas, TX 75201
Copyright © 1994 by Iza Trapani

Printed in Italy by STIGE Turin
10 9 8 7 6 5

Book production and design by Our House

Library of Congress Cataloging-in-Publication Data
Trapani, Iza.
Twinkle, twinkle, little star / retold and illustrated by Iza Trapani.
p. cm.
Summary: An expanded version of the nineteenth-century poem in which a
small girl accompanies a star on a journey through the night sky, examining both heavenly
bodies and the earth below.
Paperback edition: ISBN 1-879085-70-4: $6.95
1. Stars—Poetry. 2. Children's poetry, American.
[1. Stars—Poetry. 2. American poetry.] I. Taylor, Jane, 1783-1824.
Twinkle, twinkle, little star. II. Title
PS3570.R336T93 1994
811'.54—dc20   93-33635
                                           CIP
                                           AC

For Aimee, Kyle, Rebecca, and Sophie—
some of the brightest little stars I know.

Twinkle, twinkle, little star,
How I wonder what you are!
Up above the world so high,
Like a diamond in the sky.
Twinkle, twinkle, little star,
How I wonder what you are.

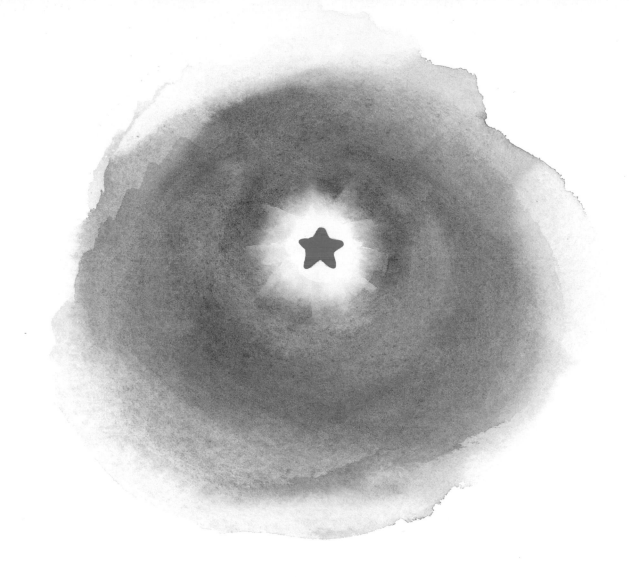

Twinkle, twinkle, star so bright,
Winking at me in the night.
How I wish that I could fly,
And visit you up in the sky.
I wish I may, I wish I might,
Have the wish I wish tonight.

Little child, your wish came true,
Here I am right next to you.
I'll take you on a magic ride,
So come with me—I'll be your guide.
There's so much that you'll see and do,
On this adventure made for you.

Out your window, through the sky
Up above the world we'll fly
Higher than a bird would go
To place where rockets go
Beyond the planes that zoom on high
Is where we'll travel, you and I

Look around you, little one,
There's the moon and there's the sun.
See the planets—count them all,
Some are big and some are small.
Can you name them one by one,
As they orbit 'round the sun?

Your planet Earth is such a sight,
I look at her with great delight.
When half the earth is in the sun,
The other half I glow upon.
For it's my job to twinkle bright,
On everyone who needs my light.

I shine on ships lost out at sea,
They know they can depend on me.
For even on the darkest nights,
I guide them to their harbor lights.
And lonely travelers wandering free,
Will find their way back home with me.

Everywhere I look below,
I shed my light and cast a glow.
Over cities, over farms,
On babies held in loving arms.
How I love to watch them grow,
As I shine on Earth below.

Little child, look down with me,
And tell me, tell me, what you see.
I see puppies in their bed,
A pony resting in his shed.
Little birds high in a tree,
And sleepy children just like me.

Yes, it's late—we can't pretend,
Our magic journey has to end.
I'll take you home, back to your bed,
You'll see me twinkling overhead.
But don't be sad—I do intend,
To shine on you each night, my friend.

Twinkle bright, my little star,
Watch me safely from afar.
Thank you for this magic night,
And the comfort of your light.
Twinkle, twinkle, little star,
What a special star you are!

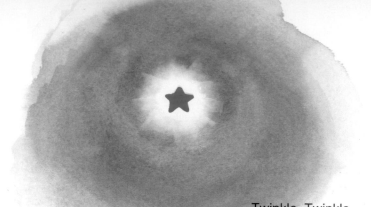

Twinkle, Twinkle

Twin - kle, twin - kle, lit - tle star, How I won - der what you are!

Up a - bove the world so high, Like a dia - mond in the sky.

Twin - kle, twin - kle, lit - tle star, How I won - der what you are.

2. Twinkle, twinkle, star so bright,
   Winking at me in the night.
   How I wish that I could fly,
   And visit you up in the sky.
   I wish I may, I wish I might,
   Have the wish I wish tonight.

3. Little child, your wish came true,
   Here I am right next to you.
   I'll take you on a magic ride,
   So come with me—I'll be your guide.
   There's so much you'll see and do,
   On this adventure made for you.

4. Out your window, through the sky,
   Up above the world we'll fly.
   Higher than a bird would go,
   To places only rockets know.
   Beyond the planes that soar up high,
   Is where we'll travel, you and I.

5. Look around you, little one,
   There's the moon and there's the sun.
   See the planets—count them all,
   Some are big and some are small.
   Can you name them one by one,
   As they orbit 'round the sun?

6. Your planet Earth is such a sight,
   I look at her with great delight.
   When half the earth is in the sun,
   The other half I glow upon.
   For it's my job to twinkle bright,
   On everyone who needs my light.

7. I shine on ships lost out at sea,
   They know they can depend on me.
   For even on the darkest nights,
   I guide them to their harbor lights.
   And lonely travelers wandering free,
   Will find their way back home with me.

8. Everywhere I look below,
   I shed my light and cast a glow.
   Over cities, over farms,
   On babies held in loving arms.
   How I love to watch them grow,
   As I shine on Earth below.

9. Little child, look down with me,
   And tell me, tell me, what you see.
   I see puppies in their bed,
   A pony resting in his shed.
   Little birds high in a tree,
   And sleepy children just like me.

10. Yes, it's late—we can't pretend,
    Our magic journey has to end.
    I'll take you home, back to your bed,
    You'll see me twinkling overhead.
    But don't be sad—I do intend,
    To shine on you each night, my friend.

11. Twinkle bright, my little star,
    Watch me safely from afar.
    Thank you for this magic night,
    And the comfort of your light.
    Twinkle, twinkle, little star,
    What a special star you are!